Messy Bessey's School D

By Patricia and
Fredrick McKissack

Illustrated by Dana Regan

Children's Press®
A Division of Grolier Publishing
New York · London · Hong Kong · Sydney · Danbury, Connecticut

To all the kids who made this title their first choice
—P. and F. M.

To Tommy and Joe
—D. R.

READING CONSULTANT
Linda Cornwell
Learning Resource Consultant
Indiana Department of Education

Visit Children's Press® on the Internet at:
http://publishing.grolier.com

Library of Congress Cataloging-in-Publication Data
McKissack, Patricia.
Messy Bessey's school desk / by Patricia and Fredrick McKissack ; illustrated by Dana Regan.
p. cm. — (A rookie reader)
Summary: When Messy Bessey starts to clean up her desk at school, she inspires the rest of the class to clean up the entire room.
ISBN 0-516-20827-6 (lib. bdg.) 0-516-26361-7 (pbk.)
[1. Orderliness—Fiction. 2. Schools—Fiction. 3. Stories in rhyme.] I. McKissack, Fredrick. II. Regan, Dana, ill. III. Title. IV. Series.
PZ8.3.M224Me 1998
[E] —dc21
97-13837
CIP
AC

Printed in the United States of America
1 2 3 4 5 6 7 8 9 10 R 07 06 05 04 03 02 01 00 99 98

Messy, Messy Bessey,
your school desk is a mess.

There's wadded-up tissue
and paper clips,
colored markers
with dried-out tips,

an old sack lunch,
a forgotten note,
scissors, tape, and
a poem you wrote.

Your desk is so messy, Bessey.
See broken crayons, pencils, too,
library books that are overdue,

DO
MY
1+1=2
2+2=4
4+4=8
8+8=16
10+10=20

rubber bands
and an apple core,
late homework
and so much more.

Messy Bessey had to agree.
Her desk was a disgrace.

So she threw away
the useless things, and
straightened out her space.

Bessey's desk was tidy now,
but something wasn't right.

AMY
FOR

There were other messy desks that were a terrible sight.

VOTE TODAY
AMY

Come on, everybody.
Let's clean up your desks, too.

Bessey got the trash can
and showed them what to do.

Lauren
for
President

Class election toda

Now all our desks are neat and clean.
Our papers and books are straight.

With everybody helping,
our classroom looks just great.

Class election
Lauren
for

Cheers, Miss Bess!

Your leadership was excellent.

That is why we elected you
to be class president.

PRESIDENT

About the Authors

Patricia and Fredrick McKissack are freelance writers, editors, and owne of All-Writing Services, a family business located in Chesterfield, Missou They are award-winning authors whose titles have been honored with th Coretta Scott King Award, the Jane Addams Peace Award, and the Newbery Honor. Pat's book *Mirandy and Brother Wind,* illustrated by Jerr Pinkney, was a 1989 Caldecott Honor Book.

The McKissacks have written three other Rookie Readers about Mess Bessey—*Messy Bessey, Messy Bessey's Closet*, and *Messy Bessey's Garden*. They have three grown children and live in St. Louis County, Missouri.

About the Illustrator

Dana Regan was born and raised in northern Wisconsin. She migrated south to Washington University in St. Louis, and eventually to Kansas City, Missouri, where she now lives with her husband, Dan, and her sons, Joe and Tommy.